My animals

BY WILLIAM H. ARMSTRONG
ILLUSTRATED BY MIRKO HANÁK

DOUBLEDAY & COMPANY, INC., Garden City, New York
1974

My Animals

Green Meadow wept and her dewdrop tears dripped from leaf to leaf and fell upon the ground. She called to her mother, Nature, in her sadness, and Ground Breeze carried her message of sorrow.

"Why have my beautiful spotted cows and my snow-white sheep been taken away? I was the envy of all the land in Wide Valley, for I was the most beautiful of all."

Mother Nature heard her child's sorrowful voice in Ground Breeze and sent West Wind to answer.

"Unpredictable Man has taken away your beautiful spotted cows and your snow-white sheep. But do not weep. I will send you a collection of my animals and you will love them for their beauty, their service, and their mystery. I will have them say to you the reasons for their presence and you will not be sad. Speak to them. They will tell you why I have sent them."

ISBN: 0-385-02836-9 Trade ISBN: 0-385-05506-4 Prebound

Library of Congress Catalog Card Number 73-81411

92186

Rabbit

Green Meadow spoke to Rabbit as he nibbled on a leaf of red clover.

"Did Mother Nature send you?"

Rabbit sat up with ears erect and answered, "Indeed. Mother Nature sent me to you. She said, 'Green Meadow is lonely because her cows and sheep are gone. Go and bring some life back to her.'

"I have built my hutch and will raise four litters of babies a year. Soon you will have more rabbits than the cows and sheep that ever grazed here.

"I will bring joy to you too. When boys come to fish in the brook which circles you like a waistband, they will laugh with glee when I scamper away. You will hear the laughter of little girls when they follow my white tail bobbing in the air. They fear me not at all. They only love me and call me by name—Peter Rabbit, Bugs Bunny, or Alice's Rabbit. You will love me because of their love for me."

Fawn

"What is this that moves in the midst of my blooming daisies?" asked Green Meadow as she took a closer look.

"I am a baby deer, called Fawn," came a small soft voice. "I am gentle and need much protection while I am still young. So my mother tells me to rest in the sun among the daisies. The color of my coat in the sunlight and my white spots blend with the daisies and I am hard to discover here. My mother has taught me to be very brave and not to run away unless I am absolutely sure that I have been discovered."

"But what will you do for me?" asked Green Meadow.

"You yearn for beauty which you thought was lost. Watch in the moonlight tonight as I graze with my mother. Listen, and you will hear Night Breeze whispering, 'Peace is beautiful. Mother Deer and Fawn have brought peace to Green Meadow.'"

Pheasant

"What's this?" asked Green Meadow. "A spot of rainbow come to earth and strutting through the wild-rose hedge and brome grass?"

"I have more colors than the rainbow," Pheasant answered as he raised his head proudly and arched his mottled golden tail feathers. "Mother Nature asked me to come to you. But I had to wait, as you can see, until the Little Blue and Indian brome grasses had grown tall enough to wave their blue and golden blades to give me ground cover to hide me from my enemies.

"But I bring you more than beauty. I bring you service too. I will eat six thousand wild-rose seeds a year and grind them in my crop so that plants cannot grow from them. If all these seeds grew into new plants, soon you would no longer be Green Meadow. You would be Thorny Thicket, shunned by all. So you see, I bring you beauty in looks, proud dignity in walking, and noble service in living with you."

Fawn's Father

"Eyes brighter than those of either a spotted cow or docile sheep are watching me from where the thistles bloom and the wild grapevine creeps. Whose eyes are these?" Green Meadow asked as she noticed also a pair of great horns half hidden amid the wild growth.

"I am Fawn's father, the Stag. I have come to live at your sheltered edge. I will browse on the tree sprouts which would grow quickly into a forest if I had not come. Mother Nature said to me that I should live here and bring my Does to graze at twilight so that you may remain a meadow."

"But why do you hide your horns in the undergrowth?" asked Green Meadow, thinking what graceful nobility was going unseen.

"I polish them on tree trunks in the forest. When I came from the shade of the forest into the sun, I found that I had polished them too brightly. I can see the sun reflected off the shiny gun barrel of my enemy, the hunter. I'm afraid he could find me the same way."

Badger

"Why do laughing boys no longer come to frolic on my green carpet or fish in the stream? Why do little girls no longer come to gather my many-colored flowers and weave them into coronets?" Green Meadow called pleadingly to Mother Nature.

"They have been scared away by snakes—poisonous ones, Cottonmouth Moccasins and Copperheads—that have found you a place to live in without fear of being trampled since the spotted cows and sheep have been taken away," Mother Nature replied. "But I will help you. I will send Badger to live with you. You will not like Badger when you first see him. He is bowlegged and pigeon-toed. His grizzled coat and his black-and-white face, with his teeth always showing, are frightening to look at. But he is wise and gentle except in his pursuit of your dreaded snakes, asking only to be left alone."

Red Squirrel

"I'm weary of the long silence," Green Meadow spoke to Mother Nature. "I miss the mooing of the cows and the bleating of the sheep. May I not have birds to sing for me?"

"The birds will come, but not yet," Mother Nature replied. "I must be sure that unpredictable man will not return with a mowing machine or plow and ruin their homes. I will send you the spendthrift tongue of the woodland, Red Squirrel, to live in the pine trees that grow along the brook. From his favorite perch on a branch not far from his cocoonlike nest, built of twigs and leaves, he will flick his tail and chatter to the dawn. His churring notes will fade to nothingness as twilight fades. He will explode with raucous scolding if Stag polishes his antlers on his pine tree. He will chatter when the boys and girls come near. He will sputter at Rabbit for nibbling wild cress at the stream's edge. He will bark and cuss at Badger and call him 'ugly.' You will nickname him 'chatterbox,' but you will never tire of him."

Wild Hog

Green Meadow studied the edge of her garment and was worried. Running-root brambles were making ragged edges. Now she knew that running-root plants sent their roots under ground in every direction and sent up shoots from bulbous buds to make new plants. If they were not stopped they would crowd out all her clover, her flowers, her Little Blue and Indian brome grasses.

"You must help me," Green Meadow called to Mother Nature.

"I will send you Wild Hog with her four Piglets," Mother Nature replied. "Wild Hog will eat the acorns that fall from the oaks where you join your neighbor, the woodland. But her Piglets do not have teeth strong enough to crack acorns. They will root out the bulbous buds from the running-roots and stop the brambles from creeping over you."

"But Wild Hogs are ugly and grimy-looking animals," Green Meadow sighed.

"But wait till you see the Piglets. I venture a guess that you will change your mind."

Wild Hog came with her Piglets and Green Meadow changed her mind. "Why, Piglets are almost as beautiful as Fawn," she said.

Red Fox

Red Fox yawned and stretched himself to his full length in the morning sun. He rolled over to warm the side that had rested on Green Meadow's dewy dampness. He tapped his beautiful bushy tail against the earth he loved. For indeed Red Fox felt that the whole earth was his playground. Even his half-closed eyes could not hide a perpetual sparkle and grin which came from a feeling deep inside himself that he lived by his wits and was free.

Green Meadow knew him well. She had seen him come and go, outwitting men on horses with dogs, men with guns and dogs, and sometimes more thoughtful men who came with dogs only to enjoy the music of the chase and at the same time admire the "old fox" who could outsmart the hounds.

Green Meadow knew that Mother Nature let Red Fox roam at will. She whispered to him as he lay in the sun, "Will you stay? There is ground cover now and plenty of fruits and berries."

"And a cottontail now and then," replied Red Fox. "And the henhouse of the man who used to drive home the spotted cows. I'll stay."

Blue Jay

"I'll have sound enough now," said Green Meadow, as Blue Jay carried dry grass to the top of one of the pine trees along the brook and wove it into a half-built nest. Then from the topmost branch came the shrill metallic call that sounded like a wheel turning on a dry axle.

"I did not send for you," Green Meadow spoke harshly, amid the noise of Red Squirrel barking, "Clown, Rascal, Nest Robber."

"But Mother Nature said it was time for me to come," Blue Jay replied in his rasping voice. "Call me all the names you wish, but one name I deserve above all others— that of Watchman. I see the hunter first and sound the alarm. And you, Red Squirrel, will be thankful for my warning call when Red-tailed Hawk soars above the nest where your babies sleep. Do those who call me Nest Robber know that for every egg I steal I eat hundreds of tree-boring beetles, caterpillars, and grasshoppers?

"Enough! I must be off to warn Pheasant that Red Fox is slipping toward him through the brome grass."

Green Meadow heaved a sigh, and suddenly Blue Jay's voice had new meaning.

Weasel

"The deadly hunters of the weasel tribe"—words to send a chill of fear over field and forest and up and down the spines of Nature's children large and small. Forever mad with the lust to kill, killing always more than they can eat, seemingly their greatest enjoyment comes from seeing blood spilled. With beady eyes afire, teeth like a razor's edge, and claws that cut with the precision of a surgeon's knife, they strike with lightning speed—a vital spot, the brain or jugular vein.

Now this chill of fear swept over Green Meadow. Blue Jay, the watchful one, found Weasel sitting on a stone at the edge of the brook, washing dried blood from his whiskers. Across Green Meadow, Blue Jay flew calling, "Weasel, Weasel! Hide, hide!"

Badger heard the call and was ashamed. For Weasel was his cousin and Badger knew well Weasel's ways. So Badger said to Green Meadow, "I know my evil cousin's ways. He will not listen to me if I ask him to leave us to our peace, although I am considered, along with Otter, the wisest and most peaceful of our family. But I know how to get him to move. I must go first into the woodland."

Porcupine

Before Weasel could begin his bloody work on Rabbit, Red Squirrel, and perhaps even Fawn and Piglets, Badger came waddling back from the woodland. Beside him, moving even more awkwardly and saying to Badger, "Slow down! What's the hurry?" came Porcupine.

Blue Jay let out his rascally, metallic call of laughter. He had seen what Porcupine could do to a whole pack of hunter's dogs, or even to Wolverine, a member of Weasel's own family—the largest member.

"Mother Nature's pincushion?" Green Meadow said to Badger questioningly.

"Oh, but more," replied Badger. "Porky loves nothing so much as peace and slow ambling through the earth. To insure him that peace, Mother Nature has equipped him with thirty thousand barbed spears. He hates violence as much as we do, but he will use his spears if violence comes.

"He came with me because I told him that only he could save us from impending violence. I also told him there were far too many willow saplings growing along the brook and that you would let him live with us and feed on them if he drove Weasel away from Green Meadow."

"He is so welcome," said Green Meadow, almost prayerfully.

So Porky ambled along the brook, through the Brome grass, under the pine trees. Wherever Weasel went, when he looked behind him, Porky was there. For a day and a night, tireless and sleepless, he followed Weasel until he drove him out of the land.

Great White Heron

Green Meadow looked at the stranger in the brook and exclaimed, "What! An Embden goose from the farmyard standing on stilts?"

"Not at all," replied the large white bird. "Both my legs and my beak are much longer than those of a goose. I am a wading bird, not a swimmer. I gather my food from the bottom of shallow ponds and brooks. I am not a diver like the goose."

"But why are you here in my small brook?" asked Green Meadow.

"Indeed your brook is small," answered Heron. "It has been growing slowly smaller without your noticing it. But Mother Nature noticed. She knew you would be sad to lose your brook, or even have it lose its sparkling dance and become a sluggish trickle. So she sent me to save it for you."

"But can you bring rain to swell it?" Green Meadow asked.

"That's not the problem," Heron replied. "There are too many crawfish. They burrow far out into the soil to hatch their eggs. They really prefer underground streams. If enough of the water that follows them finds gravel veins or crevices, your brook will go completely underground. Crawfish are lobster for me, my favorite food. So I will feast for many days and save your happy, dancing brook."

Green Meadow only sighed, for she was speechless.

Jumping Mouse

"Your short-tailed cousin, Field Mouse, I have known for a long time," Green Meadow said to long-tailed Jumping Mouse as he teetered back and forth on the tall mullen stalk as it swayed in the breeze. "But you are new here, aren't you?"

"Yes. I have been here only a little while, but I came just in time," replied Jumping Mouse in a squeaky voice. "You see, mullen and thistle seeds are my favorite food. They grow very tall and their stalks are so spiny that my cousin, Field Mouse, cannot climb up to get the seeds. I can jump to the top of the highest mullen with ease. I will eat my own weight in seeds every day. In my little tunnels under the matted grass I will store thousands of seeds, many pounds, for winter."

"Oh, I am so grateful," said Green Meadow. "If it were not for you, the mullens and thistles would crowd out all my daisies, poppies, and brome grass. But why is your tail so long?"

"It balances me when I jump. Without it I would whirl over and over, miss my perch, and land on my head back on the ground."

"Mother Nature thinks of everything, doesn't she?" Green Meadow mused.

Redheaded Woodpecker

"Queer, queer, quee-o" rang out as a red, white, and blue-black speck soared in undulating flight across Green Meadow and came to rest in the gnarled white birch, which added variety to the green of the pines that bordered Green Meadow's brook.

Then began the tap-tap-tap as Redhead circled the tree from top to bottom and back again. At a spot halfway up the tree, he tapped, listened—tapped again, and listened. Redhead had found a hollow spot caused by water which had seeped in where a branch had been blown off years before.

Now the white bark and yellow sawdust flew amid the rat-tat-tat drilling of Redhead's stout beak. Green Meadow began to worry. "Will you not kill my beautiful birch?" she asked at last.

"I will do your tree no harm," answered Redhead. "I will make my home here among your trees. Under the bark of all your trees, there are tree-borers working to destroy them. There are sap-eating insects draining the lifeblood of your pines. Wherever you see my beak marks, you will know that I am not harming, but saving your trees."

Screech Owl

Cottontail sat deadly still in the clover. She dropped her ears so they would not show in the moonlight. Red Squirrel sank deep in his nest and covered his eyes with his tail so they would not reflect the moon's rays. Fawn and her mother raised their heads from grazing and stood motionless on the half-golden carpet strewn with dewdrops which were trying to imitate the stars. Red Fox came to a stop from his easy galloping over the land, sat on his haunches, and barked his answer to the mournful, plaintive, chilly, and screechy wail that saturated Green Meadow.

Green Meadow found the great yellow eyes looking down upon her from a tall tree. "And what do you bring to me?" she asked.

"Mystery," replied Owl. "Mystery in superstitions that have grown up about me. Mystery in omens, good and bad, that are credited to my wisdom. Mystery accompanying my movement in the night. Mystery that has power to send enchanting and shivering vibrations over the dark land."

West Wind

Green Meadow listened to Mother Nature's voice in the West Wind. "When your beautiful spotted cows and snow-white sheep were taken away, you were sad. I promised to send you beauty, service, and mystery. I have kept my promise."

And as West Wind passed over Green Meadow, she whispered as she went, "Sleep well, enjoy your peaceful dreams."

Behind West Wind the dewdrop stars danced, and all the flowers nodded their sleepy heads.